Perfectly Chelsea

Also by Claudia Mills

Dinah Forever
Losers, Inc.
Standing Up to Mr. O.
You're a Brave Man, Julius Zimmerman
Lizzie at Last
$7 \times 9 = $ Trouble!
Alex Ryan, Stop That!

Contents

Perfectly Chelsea

To all my friends at St. Paul's Church

Perfectly Chelsea

Claudia Mills

Pictures by Jacqueline Rogers

Farrar, Straus and Giroux

New York

www.fsgkidsbooks.com

Library of Congress Cataloging-in-Publication Data
Mills, Claudia.
    Perfectly Chelsea / Claudia Mills ; pictures by Jacqueline Rogers.— 1st ed.
        p.   cm.
    Summary: Nine-year-old Chelsea's experiences, which include a fight with her
best friend, making mistakes in the handbell concert, and saying goodbye to the
only church minister she has ever known, help her to accept that things change
and that people, including herself, are not perfect.
    ISBN 0-374-31244-3
    [1. Church—Fiction.   2. Perfectionism (Personality trait)—Fiction.
3. Christian life—Fiction.   4. Conduct of life—Fiction.]   I. Rogers, Jacqueline, ill.
II. Title.

PZ7.M63963Pe 2004
[Fic]—dc21

2003044061

Like an Angel

Chelsea Garing sat in church with her parents, in the fifth pew on the right, an imagined halo hovering above her neat, just-combed hair. Three of the boys from her fourth-grade Sunday school class, including Danny Repetti, were sitting directly in front of Chelsea, attempting to balance their hymnals on their heads. Chelsea tried not to look at them.

Instead of watching the boys' antics, Chelsea began folding her church bulletin into a paper fortune-teller. All the girls at school were making them. They were hard work. You had to start with a square piece of paper, for one thing, and the church bulletin wasn't square. Luckily, Chelsea was good at crafts.

"Do you have a pair of scissors in your purse?" Chelsea asked her mother. The organist hadn't started the prelude yet, so it was all right to talk or play quietly. She hoped Danny and his friends would stop clowning around once they heard the first chords of the organ. She doubted it.

"Yes, I do," Chelsea's mother said. Her purse contained everything.

Chelsea cut the bulletin into a square. She saw that she was cutting off most of the Unison Prayer, the prayer the minister had printed out for the congregation to read aloud together. That was all right. Chelsea could improvise. She knew what to pray about: the first math test of the year, which was coming up at the end of September, the goal she wanted to score in her next soccer game, Danny Repetti's teasing. She didn't need any suggestions from the minister.

"May I have a pencil?"

Her mother handed her one. Then Chelsea started folding the paper and writing out color words, numbers, and her own made-up answers to questions someone might ask the fortune-teller. When she had finished, and the fortune-teller was puffed into its cup-like, cootie-catcher shape, she turned to her mother. "Ask me a question," she said.

"Is Petey going to be good in the nursery today?"

Petey was Chelsea's three-year-old brother. Sometimes he had fun playing in the church nursery with the other toddlers; sometimes he didn't.

"Okay," Chelsea said. "Pick a color." She pointed to the four colors written on the fortune-teller: pink, purple, yellow, and green.

"Purple."

"P-U-R-P-L-E." Chelsea opened and shut the fortune-teller as she said each letter. On the "E," she opened it to reveal four numbers.

"Now pick a number."

"Seven."

"One. Two. Three. Four. Five. Six. Seven." Chelsea clicked the fortune-teller seven times. Now when she opened it, four different numbers appeared inside.

"Pick another number."

"Three."

Chelsea peeked under the number three to see what she had written there.

"Absolutely not," she read aloud, and giggled. "According to the fortune-teller, Petey will *not* be good in the nursery today."

Her mother sighed, as if suspecting this was all too true, but there was a twinkle in her eyes. Chelsea's father, seated next to her mother, gave a low chuckle.

"Now I'm going to ask it a question," Chelsea said. "Will I be beautiful when I grow up?"

She went through the fortune-telling motions again. The answer came up: Yes. Chelsea was pleased. Maybe she wouldn't always have plain old straight brown hair.

Her mother put her arm around Chelsea. "The fortune-teller got that one correct. But, honey, you know that the fortune-teller can't really tell fortunes. Only God knows what the future has in store for us. This is just a game, right?"

"I know." But it was funny how often the fortune-teller was accurate. From the nursery Chelsea could hear the distant sound of a young child wailing. Petey.

The organist began to play a soft, sad piece of music. Minor key, Chelsea guessed from her piano lessons. Probably Bach. In front of her, the boys had put their hymnals down, but they had rolled their bulletins into long sticks, with which they were now dueling.

Silently, Chelsea asked the fortune-teller another question. "Will I do a wonderful job as acolyte today?" The acolyte carried a tall candlelighter down the aisle during the opening hymn and lit the two candles on the altar. Then, at the end of the service, the acolyte marched back to the altar to put out the candles during the closing hymn. A different child was acolyte each week. This was the eleventh time that Chelsea had been the acolyte since she had first served as one back in first grade. There were a lot of children in Chelsea's church, so everybody had to take turns.

Chelsea loved being acolyte. Some kids, such as Danny Repetti, practically jogged down the aisle, wearing any old thing—jeans with holes in the knees, baggy pants half falling down. When Chelsea was acolyte, she wore a pretty dress and shiny shoes, as she was wearing today. She walked down the aisle slowly and majestically. Being acolyte was like being a bride, with all eyes upon you—better than being a bride, because you didn't have to have a groom.

As the organist played on, Chelsea clicked through her fortune. Color: green. G-R-E-E-N. Number: three. Number: two. She felt a twinge of nervousness as she lifted the paper. *Would* she do a wonderful job as acolyte today?

"No way!" said the fortune, written in Chelsea's own careful cursive.

She had thought "No way!" was a pretty funny answer when she had written it there, but now she was annoyed. Oh, well. As her mother said, the fortune-teller was just pretend; it didn't really know anything. Quickly she tried for another answer. Y-E-L-L-O-W. Number: six. Number: one. Fortune: Definitely. That was more like it.

The music ended, and the minister, tall in his flowing robes, stepped up to the pulpit.

Chelsea loved Reverend Waller. He was old, but not

too old, with thick white hair framing his wise, kindly face. Even though Chelsea knew God wasn't a person, in a body, with a robe on, she still thought Reverend Waller looked like God.

"Good morning!" Reverend Waller said.

"Good morning!" the people in the pews replied.

Then Reverend Waller told everybody to stand up and greet the folks around them. Near Chelsea's family sat Danny's parents and his two older brothers. Danny's brothers shook hands with Chelsea's parents. Chelsea glared at Danny. He glared back at her. Chelsea supposed that counted as greeting each other.

When everyone was sitting down again, Chelsea slipped out of the pew and hurried to the back of the church to get ready for her big moment as acolyte. While Reverend Waller made his announcements, Chelsea imagined herself walking down the aisle in solitary splendor.

On a table in the back of the church, Chelsea found another copy of the bulletin. This one hadn't been folded into a fortune-teller with the Unison Prayer cut

off. She checked the opening hymn; it was one of her favorites, "Love Divine, All Loves Excelling."

When Reverend Waller stopped talking, the organist began playing the opening bars of the hymn. One of the ushers, Mr. Cruz, handed Chelsea a long brass candle-lighter and lit the wick for her. Mr. Cruz was Chelsea's favorite usher. He was an older man, with thick gray hair and bushy gray eyebrows and a kind, sad smile. The smile was sad because his wife, who sometimes sang solos in the choir, was sick with cancer.

Chelsea stood up extra-straight and tried to put a holy expression on her face, to look as much like an angel as she could. In time with the music, she started down the long center aisle.

"Love divine, all loves excelling, joy of heaven, to earth come down."

Chelsea didn't sing, even though she knew the words by heart. She didn't glance to the left or to the right, to see if the old ladies were smiling at her and noticing how much better an acolyte she was than Danny Repetti had been last Sunday. She gazed straight ahead at her candlelighter.

That was when she noticed that the flame had gone out.

She closed her eyes for a fleeting second, then opened them and checked again. The flame was definitely out. There was no flicker, no spark, no wisp of smoke, nothing at all.

Chelsea froze in place. She couldn't keep walking down the aisle with an unlit candlelighter. It would be too ridiculous. What would she do when she got to the altar? Pretend to light the candles?

But she couldn't turn back. She had never seen any other acolyte turn back halfway through the opening hymn. It would spoil the whole effect. It would spoil everything.

She couldn't just stand there, in the middle of the aisle, either. The congregation was already up to the second verse: "Breathe, O breathe thy loving Spirit into every troubled breast!"

If only the Holy Spirit could breathe one little flame into Chelsea's one little wick!

She saw her mother and father, twisting around in their pew to smile at her. In what she hoped would be a secret code, she gave a quick, desperate nod at her candlelighter, so that her mother alone would see what was wrong. Her mom mouthed something at her, but Chelsea couldn't tell what it was. *Come on? Turn back?*

Turning back was the best of her bad options. Willing herself to be invisible, she spun around and walked as briskly as she could to the back of the sanctuary. The faster she went, the less time anyone would have to see her. Mr. Cruz, obviously trying not to smile, lit her candlelighter again. It had better stay lit this time.

"Come, Almighty, to deliver . . ."

Chelsea started down the aisle again. Desperate this time, she tried to make herself even more angel-like than before, her steps more stately and majestic, her thoughts more firmly fixed on the golden cross hanging over the altar. She glanced at her flame: thank goodness, it was still there.

She heard some stifled laughter. It sounded like Danny Repetti. Chelsea forced herself not to burst into tears, drop the candlelighter, flame and all, and flee to the parking lot. She managed to keep putting one foot in front of the other.

Finally, as the last stanza was beginning, she reached the altar. Standing at the pulpit, Reverend Waller smiled down at her. His smile said, "You are an amazing acolyte, Chelsea Garing, with great courage and presence of mind! How fortunate we were that *you* were the acolyte on this day when disaster struck!"

Chelsea smiled back at him. He made her feel that the fortune-teller *had* been wrong the first time, and she had done a wonderful job as acolyte, after all. She loved him more than ever.

With trembling hands, she lit first one candle, then the other, and turned to retrace her steps.

Out of the corner of her eye, she saw Danny grinning at her, cross-eyed, as she marched toward him on her way back up the center aisle. "Saint Chelsea," he hissed at her.

Chelsea knew he meant the nickname for an insult. She decided to take it for a compliment. Her head held even higher, her "halo" even brighter, Chelsea marched on past Danny Repetti, ignoring him completely.

The Good Samaritan

"All right, boys and girls!" Mrs. Taylor called to the class one crisp Sunday morning in October. Mrs. Taylor was Chelsea's Sunday school teacher. Her voice was always a little too loud and hearty, as if she was trying to convince the children that the activities she had planned for that day were going to be extra-special, super-duper fun. "Today we are going to be acting out the story of the Good Samaritan!"

The other five children in the class, who had been pelting each other with beanbags from the toy box, sat down in their seats around the table. Chelsea was already seated there. She had been helping Mrs. Taylor put the caps back on all the marker pens in the crafts box. It was so satisfying to find an orange marker without a cap and an orange cap without a marker and put them together again.

Now she turned her thoughts to the play. She tried to remember what she knew about the Good Samaritan. He had rescued some man from a ditch, and Jesus had told everyone to be like him. When Mrs. Taylor was choosing the cast, Chelsea would ask to be the Good Samaritan.

"One day a man was walking down the road to Jericho," Mrs. Taylor began. She took out her big map of Bible-time places and pointed to the city of Jericho. "Who would like to be the man in our play?"

Was the man the Good Samaritan? Chelsea wasn't sure. But all the others were waving their hands, so Chelsea took a chance and raised hers, too.

Maybe because she had worked so hard on the markers, Mrs. Taylor picked her. "Chelsea, you may be the man. Danny, from now on, please don't wave your hand in front of other people's faces. Does anyone know what happens next?"

Chelsea didn't. But sooner or later she was bound to rescue the man, and then Jesus would appear and say to all the other people hanging around, "Go, and do likewise," meaning, "Go, and be like Chelsea."

The problem, whenever they acted out Bible stories, was who would play Jesus. Chelsea especially hated when Danny did. But it seemed wrong for any of them to pretend to be Jesus. Only Reverend Waller was good enough, in Chelsea's opinion, to play that part.

"As the man was walking down the road," Mrs. Taylor continued in her overly enthusiastic, Bible-story voice, "some thieves jumped on him and robbed him and left him bleeding in a ditch."

Uh-oh. Chelsea felt the color draining from her face. She had made a terrible mistake. She wasn't going to be the Good Samaritan. She was going to be the man in the ditch. Was it too late to tell Mrs. Taylor that she didn't want to be the man walking down the road, after all?

"Of course, we won't really jump on Chelsea and knock her down," Mrs. Taylor said, smiling at Chelsea reassuringly. Chelsea forced herself to give a half-smile in return. "We're just going to pretend. I need two people to be our thieves."

Once again, all the other hands were waving frantically in the air. Only Chelsea's hand, guilt-stricken at the mistake it had made, lay limp and listless in her lap.

Mrs. Taylor hesitated. "All right, Danny, you may be one, and thank you for waving your hand so nicely this time. Amanda, you may be our other thief. *Pretend* thief," she added, smiling at Chelsea again.

Amanda was the only other girl in the fourth-grade Sunday school class. Chelsea liked her better than any of the boys, but not as much as she liked her best friend at school, Naomi. Naomi was Jewish. She went to her own religious class at the synagogue two blocks away.

Chelsea wondered if Naomi ever acted out Old Testament stories in her class. Naomi was stronger and braver than Chelsea. If two pretend thieves tried to jump on Naomi and leave her bleeding in a ditch, they'd be the ones who ended up in the ditch when Naomi was done.

"Then a priest walked by, and he saw the man in the ditch, but he didn't stop to help. He passed by on the other side of the road." Mrs. Taylor's face wore a sorrowful expression here. Clearly she had expected more of a priest.

"And then a Levite—that's like a priest—came along, and *he* saw the man in the ditch, and he didn't stop to help, either. He also passed by on the other side of the road. Who wants to be the priest and the Levite?"

The remaining three all put up their hands. Chelsea stared at them. Didn't they realize that the next part, the last part, was going to be the best part, the part of the Good Samaritan? These kids would raise their hands for anything.

Of course, Chelsea had done the same thing. That was how she had gotten stuck with the part of the man in the ditch in the first place.

Travis was chosen to be the priest, and Justin the Levite. Angus, the only one left now, looked disappointed.

"And *then*," Mrs. Taylor said, giving an extra-big

smile to Angus, "a Samaritan came along. Now, this man was not from the same country as the wounded man. He was from the country of Samaria." Mrs. Taylor pointed to the Bible-time map again. "The Samaritans and the wounded man were enemies."

Angus perked up. "So does the Samaritan jump on the guy in the ditch and beat him up some more?" he asked hopefully.

"No, Angus. This is the story of the *Good* Samaritan."

Angus's face fell again.

"Angus, as our Good Samaritan, you help Chelsea. You bandage her wounds and put her on your horse and take her to a nearby inn."

"Do I have to?" Angus asked.

Chelsea had been thinking the same thing. Almost as bad as being pushed into a ditch by Danny would be having her wounds bandaged by Angus. It was certain to tickle, and Chelsea was extremely ticklish. And what would they use for the horse?

"Can I be the horse?" Danny asked, not even bothering to wave his hand this time.

Mrs. Taylor frowned uncertainly. Chelsea knew that Mrs. Taylor hated to dampen any enthusiasm shown by the boys in Sunday school. But Chelsea also knew Danny's idea of a horse would be a bucking bronco at a cowboy rodeo.

"All right, Danny," Mrs. Taylor said, replacing her frown with a too-cheerful smile.

"Can we wear costumes?" Amanda asked.

"What a good idea!" Mrs. Taylor exclaimed.

As soon as the words were out of her mouth, Chelsea's classmates were tearing into the boxes of costumes from the Christmas pageant, which were stored in the cupboard at the back of the Sunday school room.

Chelsea slowly joined them. She pulled a coarse brown tunic over her pink Sunday school dress. She draped a square of striped fabric over her head and tied a ragged strip of brown fabric around it to hold it in place.

"All right, actors," Mrs. Taylor said, "take your places."

The thieves hid behind the battered couch in the

Sunday school room. Chelsea got ready to walk down the road to Jericho. She wished Mrs. Taylor would give everyone another reminder about how this was all just pretend and how nobody would really get pushed into a ditch. Or have their wounds tickled. Or be made to ride a bucking bronco.

Mrs. Taylor began reading the story, taken from the book of Luke in the Bible. "A man was going down from Jerusalem to Jericho, and fell into the hands of robbers," she said. "They beat him and went away, leaving him half dead."

Chelsea had just heard the alarming words "half dead" when Danny jumped out from behind the couch and hurled himself at her, with Amanda following behind.

"Remember, this is *pretend*!" Mrs. Taylor called out, but it was too late. Chelsea had already been knocked to the floor. The floor was a lot harder than a nice dusty ditch would have been. Chelsea lay there, feeling at least three-quarters dead.

"Stop it!" Angus, the Good Samaritan, was there to defend her. He yanked Danny away. "Leave her alone!"

Forgetting to pass by on the other side of the road, Travis and Justin leaned over Chelsea. Justin put out his hand to pull her to her feet. Amanda's face, beneath her Bible-time headdress, looked close to tears.

Mrs. Taylor finally managed to push through the group of fourth graders. "Are you all right, honey?" she asked Chelsea.

"I think so." Chelsea sat up slowly. She only felt a quarter dead now.

"I'm sorry," Amanda said. "Danny pushed her, not me."

"I was just acting out the play," Danny said, his face red, as all the others glared at him. "I'm sorry, too, Chelsea."

Mrs. Taylor helped Chelsea over to the Sunday school table, the other children trailing mournfully behind her. Chelsea's right side was still sore from her fall, but she took comfort in her new importance as the wounded heroine of the Sunday school play.

When everyone was seated, Mrs. Taylor said, "Well, we didn't follow the script for our play very well, but I think all of you turned out to be Good Samaritans, after all."

"Not Danny," Angus pointed out.

"Even Danny," Mrs. Taylor said kindly. "Now let's think of how we can be Good Samaritans in our real lives. Suppose someone you know is sick. What could you do to be a Good Samaritan to that person?"

Chelsea thought about Mrs. Cruz, in the choir, who had cancer. "You could make a card," she suggested.

"Excellent, Chelsea. Any other ideas?"

"You could go visit," Danny offered.

Chelsea wondered if a sick person could survive a visit from Danny.

"Excellent, Danny. Anyone else?"

Chelsea put up her hand again. "You could take a casserole." Her mother was always taking casseroles to people. Chelsea had helped her take a taco casserole to Mrs. Cruz just last week.

"Those are all good ideas," Mrs. Taylor said. "Today, in Sunday school, we don't have time to visit our church shut-ins, or bake any casseroles, but we can make cards for them. Travis, would you get the construction paper? Amanda, would you please get the markers? And we all need to thank Chelsea for doing such a good job of putting the caps back on our markers this morning."

Chelsea felt a glow of pride. She started drawing a huge vase of flowers on the front of her card for Mrs. Cruz. She loved to draw.

Danny was drawing some bulgy, gray thing on his card.

"What's that?" Chelsea asked.

"It's a B-52 bomber," Danny explained. "It's going to be dropping all these big bombs, and when each one explodes, it's going to say GET WELL SOON."

"What a clever idea, Danny," Mrs. Taylor said.

Chelsea thought it was a horrible idea. But maybe it was a clever idea, for Danny. She kept on drawing, and her flowers for Mrs. Cruz—roses, tulips, daffodils, daisies—burst into bloom.

Hanukkah Candles

Chelsea had been best friends with Naomi Goldberg since they met on the first day of kindergarten. As soon as her mother had kissed her goodbye, Chelsea had felt hot tears of fear and loneliness welling up in her eyes. And then Naomi, a complete stranger, had reached out and taken Chelsea's hand. In that moment, the two girls had become friends forever.

Chelsea and Naomi were in the same class again in first grade, but in different classes in second and third. Now they were back together in fourth. Being in class with Naomi was the best thing about fourth grade for Chelsea. Having Danny Repetti in their class was the worst. Why did Danny have to be the only kid from Sunday school who went to Lincoln Park Elementary with Chelsea?

November had arrived, and soccer season was over—Chelsea's team had won every game but one. Naomi hadn't been on Chelsea's soccer team. Naomi hated sports. When all the fourth graders had done their mile run at the high school track in October, Naomi had come in next to last. After finishing her own race, Chelsea had walked the rest of Naomi's with her, to cheer her on.

"Don't cheer," Naomi had said, panting. "It only makes it worse when people cheer."

So Chelsea hadn't cheered, not out loud. But she had held Naomi's hand as she walked her last half-lap. Just as Naomi had held her hand on the first day of kindergarten.

Now the fourth graders were doing folk dancing in P.E., indoors in the gym. Whenever a dance called for partners, Chelsea and Naomi tried to dance together. Every once in a while, Chelsea wished she could be partners with someone who could tell her left foot from her right. Only for a second, though. She would still rather dance with Naomi than with anybody else.

On the Monday before Thanksgiving break, Mrs. G. blew her whistle to get everyone's attention. "So far we've learned folk dances from Spain, Greece, and Jamaica. Today we're going to learn a folk dance from Israel."

"Maybe you'll be good at this one," Chelsea whispered to Naomi. Naomi had spent last summer in Israel with her family.

"I won't," Naomi whispered back.

"Has anyone ever been to Israel?" Mrs. G. asked the class. "Does anyone have a Jewish family tradition?"

Every winter, Chelsea's school celebrated everybody's family traditions. Being Christian, or Jewish, or Muslim wasn't a religion at Lincoln Park Elementary School—it was a family tradition.

Naomi raised her hand, along with two others.

"Good!" Mrs. G. said. "Come on up here, David, Leah, Naomi. You can help me demonstrate the steps of our Israeli folk dance. It's called the hora. We're going to dance it to the traditional song 'Hava Nagila.' "

Leah and David joined Mrs. G. at the front of the gym. Naomi didn't.

"Naomi?"

Naomi shook her head. Mrs. G. hesitated. Then she turned to David and Leah. "All right, you two. Face the class and join hands."

As David's and Leah's hands touched, someone giggled. Chelsea hoped with all her heart that there weren't any Christian folk dances that she and Danny would have to do together. She didn't think she would be brave enough to say no to Mrs. G. Though if she had to choose between saying no to Mrs. G. and holding hands with Danny Repetti, maybe she'd find deep inside her a well of bravery she had never known she possessed.

Mrs. G. switched on her tape player. Still holding hands, David and Leah nimbly did the steps Mrs. G. told them to. The dance looked pretty hard. When the music came to an end, Mrs. G. turned to the class. "Let's give it a try," she said.

Chelsea and Naomi joined hands, to make sure they would be together. Mrs. G. looked back at David and

Leah. "Let's do something different today," she said. "In our circle, let's alternate boy, girl, boy, girl."

Chelsea's grip tightened on Naomi's hand. She hoped Naomi would be brave again and simply shake her head at Mrs. G. in polite but firm refusal. Chelsea tried practicing the same head shake herself. It didn't feel right when she did it. She said a quick silent prayer: "Please let there be two girls left over, and please let them be Naomi and me."

Suddenly Danny was there, tugging at their joined hands. "Boy, girl, boy, girl," he chanted.

"Girl, girl, girl, girl," Chelsea shot back.

To her horror, Naomi drew her hand away and let Danny take his place between them. The next thing Chelsea knew, Danny was holding on to her left hand, and another boy was holding on to her right hand.

The music began again. Chelsea danced along with it; it wasn't as if she had any choice. Soon she almost forgot she was holding hands with not one but two boys. The music was so fast Chelsea couldn't think of anything but how to move her feet. She hoped that somehow Naomi was managing to move her feet, too.

They danced the hora four more times, and then P.E. class was over. When they lined up to walk back to their regular classroom, Danny was right next to Chelsea and Naomi.

"I didn't know you were Jewish," he said to Naomi.

"Now you do," Naomi said.

"Do you have Christmas?" he asked.

"No. Do you have Hanukkah?"

"No, of course not," Danny said. "But some Jewish people have Christmas. A boy in my class last year was Jewish, and he had a Christmas tree. They called it a Hanukkah bush."

"We don't. My father doesn't believe in Hanukkah bushes."

"Why not? It's just a tree with lights and decorations on it. You don't have to be Christian to cut down a tree and stick it in your house and hang stuff all over it."

"Then why do they call it a Christmas tree?"

Chelsea was glad they were almost back at their classroom. She was so mad at Danny! How dare he try to make Naomi feel bad about not having Christmas?

But Naomi didn't look flustered. She never looked

flustered. Even when she was finishing up her mile run, she hadn't looked flustered.

"Math groups," Mrs. Campbell called out when they reached their room. As if nothing had happened, Naomi picked up her math notebook and pencil and went to join her math group. But Chelsea still felt cross and crabby: her math group had Danny in it.

"What's your problem?" Danny asked her as she icily took the only open seat, next to his, and scooted the chair as far away from him as possible.

"You know," she snapped at him.

"No, I don't."

"You're awful. Picking on Naomi like that. Saying bad things about Hanukkah."

Danny looked defensive. "I didn't say anything bad about Hanukkah. I was just asking her why she didn't have a Christmas tree. Or a Hanukkah bush. I was just *asking*."

"You were acting like Christmas is better than Hanukkah."

Danny hesitated. Then he said, "Well, don't you think it is?"

Chelsea didn't reply. She hated herself for sinking so low as to agree with Danny Repetti on anything. But this time, in her heart of hearts, she did. The good thing about Hanukkah was that it lasted eight days, and Jewish children got presents on all eight of them. The good thing about Christmas was—everything else. Christmas really did have more good things than Hanukkah did. Still, out of loyalty to her best friend, Chelsea was mad at Danny Repetti for saying so.

Naomi called Chelsea on the day after Thanksgiving. "Can you come over tonight for dinner? It's the first night of Hanukkah, and you've never been to Hanukkah at my house. I've seen your Christmas tree, but you've never seen our menorah. Tonight we're lighting the first candle, and we're having latkes for dinner—potato pancakes. With applesauce."

Latkes sounded yummy. "I'd love to come. But how can it be Hanukkah already? It's the end of November."

"Well, some years it comes early, some years it comes late."

Like Easter, Chelsea thought. Maybe that was another good thing about Hanukkah, that sometimes it came early. Chelsea wished Christmas would come early every year.

Chelsea's mother dropped Chelsea off at Naomi's at five o'clock. Naomi's house looked bare from the outside. Chelsea's house was already all decorated, with tiny white lights outlining every door and window, twinkling in every bare-branched tree. Chelsea's father had spent most of the morning up on his ladder, making sure each strand of lights was hung just so. Chelsea's family had put up their tree that afternoon, too. By contrast, Naomi's house was so plain that Chelsea felt a pang of pity for her friend.

But inside everything smelled wonderful, like potatoes and onions bubbling golden in fragrant hot oil. Chelsea suddenly realized she had never been hungrier in her life.

"Welcome, Chelsea," Naomi's father said. "Happy Hanukkah." He was wearing a small, circular, embroidered hat on his head; Chelsea knew it was called a yarmulke.

On a small table in front of a window stood the tall silver menorah, with four candleholders branching out on each side of the tall one in the middle, which held a candle. Only one of the eight smaller candleholders—one for each night of Hanukkah—had a candle in it tonight.

"Do you know the story of Hanukkah?" Naomi's father asked Chelsea.

Chelsea shook her head.

"Long ago, our people were not allowed to follow our religion. The Syrian king who ruled over us sent his soldiers to destroy the sacred oil lamp that burned in our Temple, our eternal light, our symbol of God. But brave Jewish soldiers, the Maccabees, led by a man named Judah, drove the king and his soldiers away. Then they lit the lamp in the Temple again, though they had only a little bit of oil left, just enough for one day. But the lamp burned on and on, for eight whole days, until new oil could be found. And that is the miracle we celebrate at Hanukkah."

It sounded like a pretty good miracle to Chelsea. But not as good as a baby in a manger, and a star, and

shepherds in the fields, and three Wise Men bearing gifts.

"Just a small miracle," Mr. Goldberg said, as if reading Chelsea's thoughts. "And Hanukkah is just a small holiday. Not like Yom Kippur, or Rosh Hashanah, or Passover. We make its celebration as special as possible, but Hanukkah is not to us what Christmas is to you."

Naomi's brothers appeared in the room, three tall boys, all older than Naomi. They were wearing yarmulkes, too. No wonder Naomi didn't mind touching a boy in P.E. class. She was used to boys. Chelsea just had Petey, and he didn't seem like a full-fledged boy to her yet.

They gathered around the table—Naomi's parents and brothers, and Naomi and Chelsea. Everyone recited the blessings, and Naomi's oldest brother lit the candle in the middle, then used it to light the first candle of Hanukkah.

Just these two small candles made Naomi's whole house feel bright and happy, as if God was there, in their midst. And with Naomi's family and Chelsea watching them, the two candles felt as bright as an entire Christmas tree.

Then the children opened their first-night-of-Hanukkah presents. Naomi got a fuzzy pale blue sweater. Chelsea got a present, too, from Naomi: a tiny poodle dog charm for her charm bracelet. Chelsea didn't have a present for Naomi, but she guessed that was all right. She'd give Naomi her present at Christmas. They each gave presents according to their own family traditions.

Mrs. Goldberg carried the steaming platters of latkes to the table. Chelsea took the first bite so greedily that she almost burned her mouth. It was delicious!

"So how do you like your first Hanukkah?" Naomi's father asked her. "Very different from Christmas, isn't it?"

Hanukkah was definitely different from Christmas. But it wasn't better, or worse, Chelsea decided. Just different. So Danny was wrong. Again. As usual.

Chelsea couldn't answer until she'd swallowed her big mouthful of potato pancakes. Then she said, "I like my first Hanukkah. I like it a lot."

Straw for the Manger

December brought the season called Advent in Chelsea's church. Advent wasn't Christmas, Reverend Waller explained in one of his sermons. Advent was the season of getting your heart ready for Christmas.

Chelsea felt her heart was ready for Christmas right now. But Christmas was still almost three weeks away.

That week in Sunday school, Mrs. Taylor called the children to the table. On the floor next to the table sat a wooden box. Near the box was a plastic bag full of straw. Mrs. Taylor was holding a doll, wrapped in a soft cotton blanket.

"This doll is our baby Jesus," Mrs. Taylor said, "and

the box is His manger. Our job is to get the manger filled with straw to make a nice soft bed for Him to lie in."

Danny stuck his hand into the plastic bag, pulled out a big bunch of straw, and dumped it in the box. "Ta-da!" he said.

"Put the straw back, Danny," Mrs. Taylor said in her kind, patient voice. Danny began cramming the straw back into the bag.

Mrs. Taylor went on, "Every time any of us does a good deed, we're going to take one piece of straw out of the bag and put it in the manger. Does everybody understand?"

The children nodded. As Danny continued to shove his straw back into the bag, some of it fell on the floor. Chelsea reached down and picked it up for him. She waited to see if Mrs. Taylor would count that as a good enough deed to earn Chelsea the first piece of straw for the manger. But Mrs. Taylor didn't seem to notice.

"Who did any good deeds this past week?" she asked.

Every hand was in the air, except for Danny's.

"I helped a new girl at school find the health room," Amanda said.

"Excellent, Amanda." Mrs. Taylor gave Amanda one of the big, approving smiles she usually saved for Chelsea. Amanda put the first piece of straw in the manger.

"I cleaned my room," Travis said.

Mrs. Taylor hesitated, as if unsure if this was worthy of an entire piece of straw. "Did you do it on your own, or did your mother have to tell you to do it?"

"She had to tell me, but she didn't have to yell. Well, she only yelled a little bit."

"All right," Mrs. Taylor decided. "You may put a piece of straw in, too."

Travis beamed as he put one broken wisp of straw in the bottom of the manger. Chelsea thought helping Danny pick up the straw he had dropped was a much better good deed than that one.

"I helped a stray dog find its owner," Justin said.

"I helped my mother put away the groceries," Angus said. "Two eggs in the egg carton broke, but the other ones didn't."

Chelsea was glad when her turn finally came. "I did *three* good deeds," she announced, waiting to see if Mrs. Taylor would gasp with admiration.

"I played Candy Land with Petey, and I helped my teacher at school clean up the bookshelves, and I helped bake cranberry bread to take to Mrs. Cruz." The frail old lady had hugged Chelsea when she had given her the bread. That had been the best good deed of all.

"You may put three pieces of straw in the manger," Mrs. Taylor told Chelsea.

Danny scowled. "Saint Chelsea," he whispered so that Mrs. Taylor couldn't hear.

Chelsea smiled loftily.

"Danny, did you do any good deeds?" Mrs. Taylor asked.

"No," Danny muttered.

"I bet you did," Mrs. Taylor said encouragingly.

"No, I didn't."

"Were you kind to anyone at school? Did you do your chores at home? Did you walk your dog?"

Danny shook his head.

"Did you make your bed?" At this point, Mrs. Taylor was obviously trying to think of anything at all.

Danny shook his head again.

Chelsea was shocked. Danny didn't even make his bed! If you could get straws for making your bed, she should have seven more straws right now, one for every day of the week. But making your bed probably counted as a good deed only if you had done absolutely nothing else.

"Well, we're *all* going to do a good deed this morning." From beneath the table Mrs. Taylor produced an empty shoe box. "This is an empty shoe box."

"Duh," said Angus, trying to be funny.

Chelsea thought he should have to take his straw out of the basket for that. But Mrs. Taylor just ignored him. "Our Sunday school class is going to be handing out empty shoe boxes in church today. I have enough for you to give one to each family."

"Our good deed is giving people empty shoe boxes?" Danny asked.

"People in the church are going to *fill* the shoe boxes," Mrs. Taylor went on, "with gifts to give the homeless. A warm hat and gloves, a small bottle of lotion, a package of tissues, toothpaste and a toothbrush, candy or gum. They'll bring the boxes back to church, all filled and wrapped, and we'll deliver them to the homeless shelter for their Christmas Eve party."

"And we get a straw for handing out the boxes?" Travis asked.

"One each for handing out the empty boxes, and then one for filling your own box with your family, and one for helping deliver them to the homeless shelter. Our manger is going to be full pretty soon, and some homeless people will have a merrier Christmas. And then we can put baby Jesus in His manger."

. . .

On Tuesday, after school, Chelsea and Petey went with their mother to shop for things to put in their shoe box. Their mother let them buy as much as they could fit in the box, including a foil-wrapped chocolate Santa. But Petey cried when he realized that the chocolate wasn't for him. "Petey wants Santa!" he screamed, refusing to let go of the Santa he had chosen.

Their mother sighed and bought another Santa for the box, letting Petey keep the one he was clinging to. No piece of straw for Petey, Chelsea thought.

By Sunday, Chelsea had earned *eight* pieces of straw. The other children in her Sunday school class also had lots of good deeds to report, though no one had as many as she did. Danny had three: he had filled his shoe box, he hadn't punched his brother after his brother called him "Danny Doofus," and he had made his bed on Wednesday.

The following Sunday was the day to deliver the shoe boxes. Mrs. Taylor would drive one car full of kids and shoe boxes; Chelsea's father would drive another.

The children in Chelsea's class began taking stacks of boxes to the two cars. Chelsea carried her box very carefully. It was the most beautiful of all, wrapped in shiny red paper, with a huge silver bow. She made sure to put it on top of a pile so the bow wouldn't get crushed.

The boys were having a contest to see who could carry the most boxes at a time. Angus came out with a stack of five boxes. He could barely see over the top. Danny came out with a stack of six boxes. He *couldn't* see over the top. He tripped on the curb. Mrs. Taylor caught him just in time to keep him, and his tower of boxes, from falling.

"Please be careful," Mrs. Taylor said.

Chelsea and Amanda rode to the shelter with Chelsea's dad. The boys all crammed in with Mrs. Taylor. Chelsea thought Mrs. Taylor deserved two pieces of straw for that.

At the shelter, the children filed in behind the grownups to see where the shoe boxes should go. The lady at the desk led them down a long, shabby hall, past large rooms lined with bunk beds. The beds were bare—no sheets, blankets, or pretty bedspreads. Just stained mattresses. The shelter smelled funny. Chelsea wrinkled her nose.

"It's disinfectant," Chelsea's dad told her.

There were no homeless people at the shelter during the day. Chelsea wondered where they went and what they did all day long. It was cold outside. And

Chelsea's homeless person didn't yet have the warm hat and gloves she had packed in her shoe box.

"You can put the boxes here," the lady said when they reached a small dark room at the end of the hall.

"All right, children," Mrs. Taylor said. "You can start bringing them in. No running!" she added as the boys pelted past her.

Chelsea hurried to the car to get her first load of boxes. Halfway down the hall, Danny raced toward her with an even taller stack. Before she had time to shout a warning, he ran right into Chelsea.

Danny fell down, Chelsea fell down, and the boxes went flying everywhere. Chelsea saw one of them hit the wall next to her. It was shiny and red, with a huge silver bow on top.

"That's my box!" Chelsea cried. Almost in tears, she scrambled to her feet and hurried to pick it up. The shiny red paper was torn. The huge silver bow was bent.

Chelsea couldn't hold back her tears. "You ruined it!" she shouted at Danny. "You ruined my box!"

Danny started picking up the other boxes. The shelter lady put her hand on Chelsea's shoulder. "I have some tape in my office. We can fix that so it'll look almost as good as new."

Almost. Shiny paper would look horrible with tape all over it. And tape couldn't fix a crumpled bow.

"Danny was just trying to help by carrying as many boxes as he could," Mrs. Taylor said. "Right, Danny?"

Danny didn't answer.

I hate you, Danny Repetti, Chelsea wanted to shout at him. But she couldn't, not with Mrs. Taylor right there.

The box looked a little bit better when the shelter lady was finished with it, but not a lot better. Chelsea was still sniffling as she stuck it in a dusty corner of the storage room. It didn't matter if ten other boxes got piled on top of it now.

"Chelsea," Mrs. Taylor said when the others had gone back to get the final load. "Bringing gifts to the homeless is a very good deed. But being kind to someone who has made a mistake is a good deed, too."

Before Chelsea could say anything, Danny came

quietly down the hall. He was carrying just four boxes this time.

Danny had made a mistake when he dropped the shoe boxes. Chelsea was supposed to be kind to him. She forced a smile. "You carried in an awful lot of boxes, Danny," she said grudgingly.

He gave a big grin. "Twenty-seven in all!"

He looked so pleased at the compliment that Chelsea felt glad she had been kind.

Back at church, each of the children put another piece of straw in the basket. Had Mrs. Taylor meant that Chelsea could put in *two* pieces of straw, one for helping with the boxes and another for smiling at Danny? Chelsea didn't think so. But she had nine other good deeds to help fill the basket.

• • •

On Christmas Eve, Chelsea came to church with her parents and Petey. She saw Danny there with his family, too.

In the front of the church, baby Jesus lay in His comfy manger, on a thick bed of straw. Downtown at the homeless shelter, somebody was opening Chelsea's shoe box. She hoped he didn't mind if his bow was a little bit crumpled. Danny hadn't meant to crumple it.

The service began.

"Angels we have heard on high sweetly singing o'er the plains," Chelsea sang joyously.

Chelsea's heart was ready for Christmas.

Make a Joyful Noise

Usually January was a letdown after Christmas: cold, gray, with no Christmas lights anywhere. But this year Chelsea was excited about January, because the church was starting a brand-new youth bell choir for any children who wanted to be in it.

Chelsea was the first one there, at the first practice, on the second Wednesday evening in January. The shiny bells, gleaming invitingly, were laid out in order of size on long tables covered with thick foam rubber.

"Welcome, Chelsea!" Mrs. Phillips greeted her. Mrs. Phillips directed the adult bell choir, too. She was tiny and bright-eyed, like a bird. "I'm so glad you're here to play bells with us."

Chelsea watched the other new bell ringers as they arrived. They were mainly middle school kids, plus some fifth graders. Chelsea was the only fourth grader, and there were no younger kids at all. Bell ringing must be too hard for second and third graders. It was too hard for all but the most grownup and serious fourth graders, Chelsea thought with satisfaction.

Then the door of the bell choir room burst open. In raced Danny Repetti. "Did you pick the bells yet?" he shouted. "I want to play the real humongous ones!"

"Welcome, Danny," Mrs. Phillips said with a big smile. "You're just in time. I'm going to assign the bells right now."

Just in time was five minutes late, Chelsea noticed. But she didn't care if Danny got the huge bells at the far table. Any bell would probably sound awful with Danny playing it.

Suddenly Chelsea remembered that she was supposed to be kind to Danny despite his faults. But it was hard to hold on to a Christmas heart all the way into January.

When Mrs. Phillips assigned the bells, Chelsea got three: a C bell that Mrs. Phillips said was the same as middle C on the piano keyboard, the D right above it, and a bell in between that could be either C sharp or D flat, depending on what the music called for.

Chelsea looked at Danny. He had three bells, too, all enormous. But he didn't have middle C. From her piano lessons Chelsea knew that middle C was the most important note on the whole piano. It was probably the most important note in the bell choir, too.

Just then there was a terrible bonging crash. Danny had dropped one of his huge bells on the thinly carpeted floor.

"Danny!" Mrs. Phillips almost shrieked. It sounded as if she was also having trouble reacting kindly to Danny's faults.

Then she got her friendly smile back in place again. "That's all right. I forgot to tell you how *expensive* and *fragile* these bells are. They look solid and sturdy, don't they? But they can break very easily. And you're going to need to wear white gloves when you handle the bells. The oil from your hands can tarnish the brass."

Chelsea felt proud as she put on her white cotton gloves. She was never going to drop *her* bells. If middle C broke, that would probably be the end of the bell choir, until they could get it fixed.

Mrs. Phillips showed the children how to hold their bells in front of their chests, with the handle down and the bell pointing up, and how to ring them, by snapping their wrists forward.

Chelsea loved the sound of her bells, of everyone's bells, ringing together. People always said that angels in heaven played harps. Chelsea thought they must play harps *and* bells.

"Open your music now to the first piece I have for you," Mrs. Phillips said, " 'Joyful, Joyful, We Adore Thee.' " It was one of Chelsea's favorite hymns.

On Chelsea's music, all of her C's were circled in red; her D's were circled in blue. She had one C sharp to play; it was circled in green.

They began to play "Joyful, Joyful, We Adore Thee," very slowly at first. At least, they began playing *something*. It didn't sound at all like the hymn in the hymnal. Was this one of those songs that had the same words but different tunes?

"Marie, you should be playing your F *sharp*," Mrs. Phillips said. "Sara, play out more—we have to be able to hear the melody. One, two, three, four, 'Joyful, joyful, we adore thee . . .' "

It sounded more like the regular hymn this time.

Even though they weren't as big as Danny's, Chelsea's bells were pretty heavy. Her arms began to ache from ringing. And Chelsea kept forgetting to play her one C sharp. That measure definitely didn't sound right, played with C instead.

When the practice was over, the children helped to put the bells back in the special padded cases. Each bell had a soft velvet compartment just its shape and size. Chelsea felt as if she were tucking her bells into bed as she laid them carefully in their places.

In the scramble to get all the bells put away, Danny

dropped his biggest bell again. Mrs. Phillips winced, but she didn't yell this time.

"Oops," said Danny.

The next practice went more smoothly. Mrs. Phillips taught the children other ways to ring the bells. You could thump your bell on the foam-padded table. You could reach inside and pluck the little metal thing in the middle. You could tap it with a tiny mallet. You could swing it back and forth in a long slow arc.

Chelsea's bells sounded wonderful if she played the right bell at the right time. But they sounded terrible if by mistake she picked up her C bell instead of her D bell, and worst of all if, instead of her C bell, she picked up her C sharp. And she had to switch the bells so quickly that it was easy to make a mistake.

. . .

"Bell ringing is hard," Chelsea said to Naomi that weekend, while they were stringing beads for bracelets at Naomi's house. The fortune-teller fad was over, and all the girls were making bracelets now.

"I bet you're good at it, though," Naomi said. "You're good at piano."

"Piano's different," Chelsea said. In piano the keys stayed put. The C key and the D key on the piano didn't surprise you by changing places. And the sharp and flat keys were a completely different color, so you couldn't possibly get them mixed up with the regular keys.

Chelsea tried on a bracelet of pink and yellow beads. She held up her arm and twirled it back and forth to admire the way it looked. When she wore jewelry, she felt like a princess.

"Put yours on, too," she told Naomi. "Oh, Your Highness looks beautiful tonight, in her royal jewels."

Naomi giggled. "I don't think princesses wear jeans and sweatshirts and tennis shoes."

"Some do," Chelsea said confidently. "Oh, guess who always drops his bells at bell choir practice? I'll give you three guesses."

"One, Danny Repetti. Two, Danny Repetti. Three, Danny Repetti."

"How did you guess?"

Chelsea took off her pink-and-yellow bracelet and tried on a red-and-blue one. "The red beads are rubies, and the blue beads are sapphires," she said.

She would wear it to church next Sunday, when the youth bell choir played during the service. Oh, she hoped she wouldn't pick up her C-sharp bell by mistake! And she hoped Danny wouldn't drop his bells on the floor.

•   •   •

As soon as church began on Sunday, Chelsea checked the church bulletin. The bell anthem followed prayer time. That was good. Chelsea could pray that she would play the right bells. She looked down at her ruby-and-sapphire bracelet glowing on her wrist. The red of the rubies matched the soft red velvet of her new dress. But looking pretty wouldn't make up for playing the wrong bell.

The first part of the service dragged. Chelsea wished the bell anthem were already over with.

Finally it was time for the youth bell choir to take their places at the special tables set up in the front of the church. Danny looked nervous, too. Chelsea bet he was going to be holding on to his bells good and tight today.

Mrs. Phillips raised her hands. "One, two, three, four," she mouthed to the bell choir.

Chelsea started ringing her D bell. She had never felt more terrified in her life. But the music sounded all right so far. Chelsea's bracelet glittered as her bells pealed forth. *Melt the clouds of sin and sadness.* Chelsea sang silently, trying to give herself confidence. Her C sharp was coming soon. *Drive the dark of doubt away.*

Oh, no. She had rung her C bell instead of her C sharp! It sounded horrible. Beyond horrible. For a moment Chelsea was so overcome with shame that she felt paralyzed, unable to go on.

She looked down at her music, then looked back up at Mrs. Phillips. Where were the rest of them in the song? They must be at least a measure ahead. Which bell should she be ringing? The C? The D? Neither?

Wait! Chelsea wanted to shout to Mrs. Phillips. *I'm lost! Wait for me!*

But the others kept going. For the rest of the piece,

desperate, Chelsea alternated between ringing her D bell and her C bell, and just ringing nothing at all. Whatever she did sounded wrong.

It was over. To her shocked surprise, people in the congregation were clapping. Didn't they have *ears*? Couldn't they hear how awful it had been? At least Danny hadn't dropped his bells. But Chelsea doubted people were clapping for that.

When she crept back to their pew, her mother gave her a little hug. Her father patted her knee. "Very nice, honey," her mother said.

"It *wasn't* nice!" Chelsea tried to hold her anguished scream to a whisper. "Every single note I played was wrong! Every single one!"

"It sounded nice to me," was all her mother said.

Somehow Chelsea survived the sermon and the closing hymn. Angus was acolyte. He walked too fast down the aisle, not in time with the music. But that was better than ruining the whole entire bell anthem.

How could this have happened to Chelsea—the best acolyte, the best Sunday school helper, the best good-deed-doer? How could she have made such a big mistake, and in front of the whole entire congregation? She had played worse than Danny!

After church, Chelsea still had to help put the bells away. She felt like dropping her bells and smashing them to smithereens. She didn't drop them, though. She just put them away. Forever.

Mrs. Phillips caught Chelsea as she was about to race out of the sanctuary. "What's the matter, dear?" she asked gently.

This was too much! How could Mrs. Phillips not know!

"I played horribly!" Chelsea cried. "Every single note was wrong!"

"I think we sounded pretty good, for our first time. You heard the applause afterward, didn't you? People were impressed at how much you all learned in such a short time."

"I'm never playing the bells again!"

"Oh, Chelsea." Mrs. Phillips led her to a pew and made her sit down. "Do you think God hears your mistakes?"

Well, if He wasn't completely deaf, He did.

"Do you think God is saying, 'Chelsea Garing was supposed to play a C sharp in measure eighteen, and she played a C natural'?"

Chelsea didn't answer. She had no idea what God was saying. Probably He was sitting up in heaven with His hands clapped over His ears.

"God is saying, 'Here's a girl who is trying her best to make beautiful music as a gift to me and to the whole congregation.' God doesn't hear the notes you play out loud; God hears the notes you play in your heart."

Chelsea hoped Mrs. Phillips was right.

Mrs. Phillips went on. "The Bible says, 'Make a joyful noise unto the Lord, all ye lands.' Sometimes the noise sounds like music, and sometimes it just sounds like—noise. The important thing is the joy."

"So God doesn't even care if Danny drops the bells?" Chelsea asked crossly.

Mrs. Phillips laughed. "I don't think He does. But *I* do. And this time Danny *didn't* drop them. There's cause for joy right there. Come on, Chelsea. Don't give up on the bells just yet."

The hard little knot of tears inside Chelsea started melting away. "All right," she said in a small voice.

She went back to the bell case to make sure that her C and D bells were in the right place.

There was one big smudge on Danny's largest bell. With the fingertip of her clean white glove, Chelsea wiped it away.

Prayer Time

Mrs. Cruz was very sick.

Usually when Chelsea and her mother and Petey went to drop off a casserole, or a loaf of homemade bread, Mrs. Cruz came to the door herself. She would invite them in to sit on her old couch with all the cat hairs on it; she would offer them treats that someone else from church had brought the day before. She always hugged Chelsea, and she would have hugged Petey if he had let her.

Today Mr. Cruz answered the door instead.

"How is she?" Chelsea's mother asked him in a low voice.

"Not so good," he said.

"Oh, Burt."

Then they heard Mrs. Cruz's voice from inside the house. "Chelsea? Are you here to visit me, Chelsea?" She must have recognized their station wagon from the bedroom window.

"You can go see her," Mr. Cruz said. He led the way to a small bedroom down the hall. Chelsea felt afraid. What had Mr. Cruz meant by "not so good"? Petey seemed afraid, too. Without saying a word, he slipped his hand into Chelsea's.

Chelsea's mother entered the room first. "There you are!" she said in a cheerful voice.

Chelsea and Petey followed behind. Mrs. Cruz was sitting up in bed. She was wearing a bright orange-and-yellow scarf on her head. It was crooked, as if she had tied it herself, quickly, without a mirror, when she saw them coming. The rest of her looked thinner, smaller. Her legs barely made a lump under her blanket.

"We brought you some flowers today," Chelsea's

mother said. "Burt's putting them in a vase for you. By February we're all ready for some daffodils."

Chelsea tried not to look at Mrs. Cruz's crooked scarf, but there was nowhere else to look. Then, out of the corner of her eye, she saw the cards they had made in Sunday school standing on Mrs. Cruz's bureau. She recognized Danny's card right away. His bursting bombs were certainly colorful.

Mr. Cruz came in with the daffodils. "These kind folks brought us a chicken casserole, too," he told his wife.

"I don't know how I can ever thank you," Mrs. Cruz said to Chelsea's mother.

"You don't have to thank us. We like to come and visit, don't we, children?"

"I want to go home," Petey said in his high, piercing voice.

Chelsea glared at him, but luckily the grownups laughed.

"How about my hug, Chelsea?" From the bed, Mrs. Cruz held out her withered arms.

If there was anything in the world that Chelsea did not want to do, it was walk over to that bed and let Mrs. Cruz hug her. But she couldn't be like Petey and say, "I want to go home." Things that were funny when you were three weren't funny when you were nine.

Chelsea made herself approach the bed. She didn't get a real hug. Mrs. Cruz just grabbed hold of Chelsea's hand and held it tight for a long moment, then let it go.

When they were back in the car, Chelsea's mother said softly, "Thank you, Chelsea." Then she said, "We need to pray for Mrs. Cruz every day now. More than daffodils and casseroles, she needs our prayers."

• • •

At the start of prayer time on Sunday, Reverend Waller asked, as he always did, if anyone had joys or concerns to share. Usually five or six people asked for specific prayers for themselves or their loved ones.

Chelsea had never raised her hand. She always *had* joys and concerns, but not ones she wanted to share, to say out loud in front of everybody. Today her joy was that she had gotten the best part in the fourth-grade play at school; her concern was that Danny was in the play, too, and might wreck it by tripping over something onstage or forgetting one of his two lines. Actually, since the bell-choir disaster, it had occurred to Chelsea that *she* might wreck the play by forgetting one of *her* lines. At least the play didn't have any bell ringing in it.

Danny's mother raised her hand. Was she worried that Danny might wreck the play, too?

"I have a joy *and* a concern," she said. She was smiling, so it couldn't be a very terrible concern. "The joy is for Jack, and the concern is for the rest of you." Jack was Danny's older brother, who had just turned sixteen. "Jack got his driver's license this week!"

Everybody laughed, including Jack.

Chelsea's mother raised her hand. Chelsea knew she was going to ask for prayers for Mrs. Cruz. "I know you've all been praying for Connie Cruz. I went to see her this week, and she's not doing well at all. So please keep her in your prayers."

Reverend Waller's face was sad and kind. "Yes,"

he said gently. "We need to pray for Connie and Burt."

Chelsea loved Reverend Waller so much. If anyone's prayers could make Mrs. Cruz well again, it would be Reverend Waller's.

No one else had any other joys or concerns to offer. Reverend Waller said, "Let us pray."

Chelsea closed her eyes and pressed her hands together. Reverend Waller's prayers were long, so Chelsea didn't listen to everything he said. She made up her own prayers instead. She decided not to mention the fourth-grade play. The fourth-grade play wasn't important, compared to cancer.

"Dear God, please make Mrs. Cruz get better," Chelsea whispered to herself. "Dear God, please make Mrs. Cruz get well."

"Amen," Reverend Waller finally said.

Chelsea unclenched her hands. "Amen," she whispered.

．　　．　　．

On Wednesday, after school, the phone rang. Chelsea's mother picked it up.

"Hello? . . . Oh, Arlene." Arlene was Mrs. Waller,

Reverend Waller's wife. "I'm so sorry to hear that. When did it happen?"

Chelsea tried to figure out from her mother's face what the bad news was. Was Mrs. Cruz worse? When had *what* happened? Had Mrs. Cruz fallen and gone to the hospital? Last winter there had been prayers at church for an older woman who had fallen in an icy parking lot and broken her hip.

Chelsea's mother hung up the phone. She pulled Chelsea onto her lap. Petey was upstairs sleeping. Chelsea knew that after such a long nap, he'd put up a big fight that night at bedtime.

"Mrs. Cruz died this morning, honey," Chelsea's mother said. One big tear rolled down her cheek.

Chelsea couldn't believe it. Mrs. Cruz couldn't have *died*. The whole church had been praying for her, more than a hundred people praying with all their might. In Chelsea's family alone, there had been a prayer for Mrs. Cruz every single day, with everyone holding hands around the table, to make the prayer even stronger.

"Mrs. Waller said she went peacefully," Chelsea's mother said. "This morning she took a little nap and just didn't wake up."

"Maybe she's still sleeping. Maybe she's in a coma, or something."

"No, honey."

For a minute, Chelsea leaned against her mother, letting her mother hold her. Then suddenly she was angry, as angry as she had ever been in her life. "But we *prayed*! Everyone in church. We all *prayed*."

"I know we did. And now we need to be praying for Mr. Cruz. These next weeks and months are going to be very hard for him."

What Chelsea had to say now was so terrible she didn't know if she could speak the words out loud. But she did. "I'm not praying anymore."

"Oh, Chelsea, honey."

"It doesn't do any good."

"Yes it does."

"Then why did Mrs. Cruz die?"

"Everyone has to die," Chelsea's mother said. "Mrs.

Cruz is in heaven now. Maybe God thought that was the best place for her to be." A second tear slid down her cheek.

Her mother tried to pull Chelsea into another hug, but Chelsea jerked away. She didn't want Mrs. Cruz to be in heaven. She wanted her to be here, on earth, with Mr. Cruz.

"Oh, honey, I know this is sad for you. I'm sad, too. We'll talk to Reverend Waller about it on Sunday," Chelsea's mother said gently. "Right now I need to finish making this meat loaf. And then we'll take it over to Mr. Cruz. Okay?"

Chelsea didn't think a person whose wife had just died would want a prayer *or* a meat loaf. But her mother looked so upset that Chelsea just said, "Okay."

During prayer time the next Sunday, Reverend Waller asked people to pray for Burt Cruz, and for Burt and Connie's two sons, who had flown into town for the funeral. When he said, "Let us pray," Chelsea shut her eyes and folded her hands, but she didn't pray. She felt guilty pretending; still, she didn't want to be the only one sitting with her eyes wide open during prayer time. And she wasn't going to pray.

She *almost* prayed. With her eyes squeezed shut and her nails digging into her hands, she asked God, "Why did you let Mrs. Cruz die? *Why?*" A question wasn't the same thing as a prayer. She waited to see if God would reply. But she just heard Reverend Waller's voice talking on and on, and then, at last, his "Amen."

After church, Chelsea took a cookie and some grapes from the snack table in the fellowship hall, while she waited to talk to Reverend Waller. A few minutes later he came over to where she was sitting with her family.

"Hi there, Chelsea. How's my big boy, Petey? Chelsea, your mother told me that you had some questions I might be able to help you with."

Chelsea felt shy telling a minister she was through with praying. It seemed rude to tell him to his face that his prayers were failures.

Her mother helped her out. "Chelsea was wondering why Connie Cruz didn't get well, with all of us praying for her."

"Our prayers didn't do any good," Chelsea said.

"I think they did a lot of good," Reverend Waller said.

"But not enough good, or she wouldn't have died." Then Chelsea remembered another unanswered prayer. "And last month I prayed that I'd do a good job playing the bells, and I played *horribly*."

Reverend Waller put his hand over Chelsea's. "I don't think that's how prayer works, Chelsea, that you pray for something and, just like that, you get it. You put your quarters in the vending machine, and out comes your root beer."

Well, if you didn't get what you prayed for, what was the point of prayer?

"I think," Reverend Waller went on, "that prayers are our way of talking to God. Of saying, God be with us, God be near us, God give us strength to face whatever we need to face. God gave Connie that strength, Chelsea, and now I believe He's going to give Burt that strength. Connie knew when she died that she was surrounded by God's love, and by all of our love. That's a big thing. That's a beautiful thing."

What Reverend Waller said sort of made sense. But Chelsea still thought God at least could have answered her little, easy prayer about the bells. And she didn't see how He could have let Mrs. Cruz die.

"If you pray never to make a mistake, that's not a prayer that God's going to answer," Reverend Waller said, as if he had read Chelsea's thoughts. "To be human is to make mistakes. Do you really want to ask God to make you not human? And here on earth death is part of being human, too."

Chelsea's next words came in a rush. "During prayer time today, I didn't really pray. I pretended. I just sat there and asked God *why* over and over again."

"That's a prayer, too," Reverend Waller said. "It's all right to get angry at God sometimes. The important thing is not to stop talking to Him. And not to stop listening for His answers."

For a moment no one spoke. Then Chelsea's mother said, "Thank you for talking to Chelsea. For talking to *us*. I needed to hear this, too."

Reverend Waller touched Chelsea gently on the head; then he went to greet the Repettis. Chelsea saw

Danny give him a huge, tackling hug. All the children loved Reverend Waller. Chelsea had heard some of the grownups saying that Reverend Waller might be moving away to take a new church, but she didn't believe it. He had to stay Chelsea's minister forever.

Chelsea felt a little better about her prayers for Mrs. Cruz now. She still didn't really understand how prayer worked. But maybe, right now, she didn't have to understand everything.

Quickly Chelsea closed her eyes and whispered, "Dear God, please take care of Mr. Cruz. Amen."

The Quarrel

Spring was slow to come. Snow fell at the beginning of March, a heavy, wet, nasty snow that refused to melt away. In Sunday school, Chelsea's class learned a song with the names of all the books of the Bible in it, and Chelsea was the best at remembering the complicated mouthfuls of unfamiliar names: Habakkuk, Zephaniah, Haggai, Zechariah, Malachi. But this didn't make her feel as proud and happy as she expected it to.

Church was depressing lately. It was Lent, the time to think about Christ's death on the cross, and all the hymns were mournful. Chelsea hated seeing the choir without Mrs. Cruz in it, knowing she would never be there again. Mr. Cruz hadn't been in church, either, since Mrs. Cruz died. Chelsea saw him only when she went with her mother to take him casseroles. He looked so much older after just a month.

Chelsea walked to school with Naomi through cold, dirty slush. At least the fourth-grade play went well; Chelsea didn't forget any of her lines, and neither did Danny. But even the success of the play couldn't make March seem less gray and gloomy.

One cloudy Friday halfway through the month, Chelsea and Naomi were eating lunch together at school, both complaining about their dental appointments, Naomi's yesterday after school, Chelsea's today. Naomi had a peanut butter sandwich; Chelsea had a ham-and-cheese sandwich. Naomi never ate ham-and-cheese sandwiches. Her family kept kosher. This meant they didn't eat meat from a pig. No ham or pork chops or bacon or pepperoni. And they didn't eat meat foods together with milk foods. No cheese-burgers.

Naomi ate half her sandwich and pushed the other half away. "I'm full," she said.

As if he had special powers of hearing, Danny appeared at their table. "Can I have the rest of your sandwich?" he asked. Danny never stopped eating, though he was as skinny as could be.

"We aren't allowed to share lunches," Chelsea told him primly. Her kind Christmas thoughts were long gone now. No one could keep kind Christmas thoughts through the month of March.

"I wasn't asking *you*, I was asking *her*," Danny said.

Naomi looked at Chelsea. "It seems silly to throw it away." She shoved the uneaten half of her sandwich toward Danny. It disappeared into his mouth in one bite.

"Did you ever hear of chewing?" Chelsea asked him.

For answer, Danny opened his mouth to display the unchewed mass of sandwich he had crammed in.

Chelsea was disgusted. "Stop it, Danny!"

"Someone told me that you're supposed to chew each mouthful a hundred times," Naomi said.

Chelsea wished Naomi hadn't said it. Danny plopped himself down on the bench next to Chelsea and started chewing with slow, exaggerated motions. "Seven, eight, nine . . ." he mumbled through the gooey lump in his mouth. With every number he spoke, Chelsea could catch another glimpse of the mashed-up sandwich. She tried looking away, pretending he wasn't there, but even the sound of his chewing was disgusting.

"Sixteen, seventeen, eighteen . . ."

"Go chew somewhere else," Chelsea told Danny.

"Twenty-one, twenty-two, twenty-three . . ."

"Count to yourself," Chelsea told Danny.

"Twenty-six, twenty-seven, twenty-eight . . ."

Chelsea didn't want the rest of her ham-and-cheese sandwich now, either. She couldn't eat while Danny was chewing. As she snatched up the unused half of *her* sandwich to carry to the trash, Danny reached out his hand.

"We aren't allowed to share," Chelsea repeated. Rules were rules. She started to get up from the table, sandwich in hand.

Danny made a grab for it. The sandwich landed on the floor, with the ham and cheese falling out of the middle.

"Mrs. Thomas!" Chelsea called.

The lunchroom lady descended on their table.

"He's trying to take my sandwich!"

Mrs. Thomas sighed. "Danny, you've had two warnings already this week. Two strikes. This makes three. You know what that means. Come with me."

Chelsea saw Danny's skinny shoulders droop as he followed Mrs. Thomas out of the cafeteria.

"That was kind of mean," Naomi said quietly.

"I know! First trying to make me throw up. Then stealing my sandwich!"

"No," Naomi said, looking down at her grapes. "*You* were pretty mean. To Danny."

"*I* was mean?" Chelsea was shocked. "*He* bothers *us*. *He* steals my sandwich. And *I'm* mean?"

"You could've let him have it. You didn't have to get him in trouble with Mrs. Thomas. Now he has to go to the office. Maybe he'll get an ISS."

An ISS was the worst possible punishment at Lincoln Park Elementary. ISS meant In-School Separation. If you got an ISS, you had to sit at a special desk all day, apart from everybody else's desks. Chelsea didn't care if Danny got an ISS. She hoped he got an ISS. If he had to eat at his own little table, no one else would have to see him chew.

Chelsea couldn't believe that Naomi was taking Danny's side. Naomi was her best friend. And Danny was *Danny*. She was afraid she was going to cry.

"Don't be mad," Naomi said. "I just feel sorry for Danny, that's all."

But Chelsea *was* mad. She couldn't help it. How could Naomi take Danny's side? How could she?

"I guess you don't want to be best friends anymore," Chelsea said, over the huge lump that clogged her throat like two unchewed sandwiches.

"Come on, Chels."

"Why would you want to be friends with someone who's *mean*?"

"Everybody's mean sometimes."

Chelsea didn't look at Naomi as she stooped to pick up her ruined sandwich. Without a backward glance, she carried her trash to the cans and stalked outside for recess.

A few minutes later she saw Naomi outside, playing jump rope with some other girls. Fine!

She didn't see Danny. He was probably sitting on the time-out bench in front of the principal's office. Unless he was at the special little ISS desk, an object of disgrace for all to behold.

Had she been mean?

It was meaner to steal someone's sandwich than to tell on someone for stealing your sandwich.

It was meanest of all to call someone mean. To call your best friend mean. When Danny had picked on Naomi about Hanukkah, Chelsea had taken Naomi's side against Danny. But now Naomi was taking Danny's side against Chelsea.

Chelsea didn't join the jump-rope game. She sat on one of the swings, without moving.

When they filed inside after recess, Chelsea was relieved to see Danny sitting at his regular desk—up front, by Mrs. Campbell, so she could keep an eye on him. He hadn't gotten an ISS, after all.

As she walked by his desk, she heard loud, fake chewing sounds. "Eighty-one, eighty-two, eighty-three," Danny was saying. Chelsea almost smiled at him. *He* wasn't mad at her, if he was still trying to drive her crazy with his chewing. *He* didn't think she was mean.

During reading time, Chelsea and Naomi usually took their books and sat on the couch together, in the back corner of the room. Today Chelsea didn't go to the couch. She saw Naomi curled up there. Their eyes met. Naomi smiled and patted the cushion next to her, as if nothing had happened. Chelsea sat stiffly at her desk, holding her book directly in front of her. Even though she was up to an exciting part in the story, she didn't read a word.

After school, the two girls usually walked home together. Chelsea lived three blocks from school; Naomi, four. But Chelsea didn't have a chance to see if Naomi still wanted to walk home with her mean former best friend. Chelsea's mother picked her up in the car, with Petey, right at three o'clock, to take them to the dentist for a checkup.

"You seem awfully quiet today," her mother said as they pulled into the parking lot by Dr. Jones's office. "Are you worried about having cavities? You've done a good job brushing since we got you your two-minute timer."

"No," Chelsea said. She'd rather have ten cavities than not have a best friend anymore.

In the waiting room, she read a *Highlights* magazine to Petey, even though it wasn't going to earn her a single piece of straw to put in the manger. A mean person wouldn't be so nice to her little brother, would she?

When her turn came, Chelsea lay in the dentist's chair and closed her eyes while Dr. Jones's assistant cleaned her teeth. "Dear God, please make me still be friends with Naomi." She prayed so hard she felt one lone tear roll down her cheek.

"Am I hurting you?" the hygienist asked, sounding surprised. "Is everything all right?"

"No," Chelsea whispered. "I mean, yes, everything's all right."

But it wasn't all right. *Dear God, please make me still be friends with Naomi.*

She thought about Naomi, about how brave she was, and funny, and bad at sports, and didn't even mind that she was bad at sports. She thought about Naomi holding her hand on the first day of kindergarten. She thought about holding Naomi's hand during the fourth-grade mile run. What would she do without Naomi?

Then Chelsea's eyes flew wide open. *Naomi* hadn't said she didn't want to be friends anymore. Naomi had said, "Don't be mad." Naomi had said, "Everybody's mean sometimes." She had saved a place for Chelsea on the couch, the way she always did. *Chelsea* had been the one who hadn't wanted to stay friends, just because one time, Naomi had thought Chelsea wasn't perfect.

Had Chelsea been mean to Danny? Was Naomi right? Danny had only wanted to be funny. And Chelsea had to admit that Danny *could* be kind of funny. It wasn't the end of the world if he took half of a sandwich that Chelsea didn't want, anyway. It wasn't worth getting someone into trouble over something that mattered as little as that. Even when he had asked

Naomi all those questions about Hanukkah, back in November, he had just said out loud the very same things Chelsea herself had been thinking. Naomi hadn't been mad at Danny then, and she wasn't mad at Chelsea now.

Naomi's a nicer person than I am, Chelsea thought.

As soon as Dr. Jones finished, Chelsea ran back to the waiting room. "Can you drop me off at Naomi's on the way home?" she asked her mother. "Oh, and I didn't have any cavities. And Dr. Jones gave me an A plus on my brushing."

Chelsea's hand shook as she rang Naomi's doorbell. Naomi hadn't been mad at her before—was Naomi going to be mad at her now?

Naomi answered the door. Without a word, the two girls rushed into each other's arms.

Chelsea had an important thought. She had prayed to God in the dentist's chair, and God had answered her. Just the way Reverend Waller said He would. She almost laughed out loud with happiness. She had prayed so many Sundays in church and never heard

God's reply, but He had just spoken to her in the dentist's chair!

"Are we still friends?" Chelsea asked Naomi, even though she knew what the answer would be.

"Friends forever," Naomi said.

Easter Sunrise

Easter was late this year, in the middle of April. Chelsea's mother baked hot cross buns, each one marked with a white icing cross on top. They took a small box of them to Mr. Cruz.

Chelsea shrank back against her mother when Mr. Cruz came to the door. He was wearing drooping pants and an old, grayish undershirt. He hadn't shaved for several days: white bristly whiskers stuck out all over his chin.

"Are you doing all right, Burt?" Chelsea's mother asked him.

"I guess so." His voice was quavery, unsteady. "It's hard. I didn't know it would be so hard."

"Come have dinner with us tonight," Chelsea's mother urged.

No, Chelsea willed him to say. *No.*

"Thanks for asking, but I don't think I'm up to going anywhere yet."

Chelsea let out her breath. She felt sorry for Mr. Cruz, but she couldn't imagine him sitting at their pretty, shiny dining room table in his undershirt, with his whiskers and the lost look in his eyes.

"That poor, poor man," Chelsea's mother said as they drove back home again.

Maybe Chelsea should make him a card, another card with blooming flowers on it. Maybe she could get Danny to make another card with bursting bombs. But right now it seemed that all the cards and all the casseroles in the world weren't going to do any good.

"Can we say a prayer for Mr. Cruz again in church this Sunday?" Chelsea asked her mother.

"Of course we can," her mother answered.

. . .

The Sunday before Easter was Palm Sunday. There was always the same opening hymn, "Hosanna, Loud Hosanna, the Little Children Sang!" During that hymn, the Sunday school children marched in carrying bunches of palms to give to all the people in the congregation. This year Petey was big enough to march, too. Chelsea waited with him at the back of the church, holding tightly to his hand.

Mrs. Taylor was there, with the other Sunday school teachers, handing out the palms to the children.

"Danny hit me with his palms!" Angus called out.

"Danny, the palms are not for hitting," Mrs. Taylor said, without even turning around to look.

"I didn't hit him with them. I was just holding them, and he bumped into me."

"Angus, try to be more careful," Mrs. Taylor said.

"I *was* careful. He whacked me with them on purpose!"

Mrs. Taylor finally turned around and glared at the two boys. "Both of you. Do I need to take your palms away and give them to someone else to carry?"

Chelsea giggled. She and Amanda were ready to carry extra palms if the boys lost their palm-carrying privileges. But she had a feeling that the real Palm Sunday had been a noisy, joyful time, as the excited crowds surged forward in their eagerness to welcome Jesus when He made His triumphal entry into Jerusalem. The boys back in Bible times had probably whacked one another with their palms, too.

The organ began playing. "Hosanna, loud hosanna," the people sang. Danny and Angus gave each other one last whack for good measure, and all the children started down the aisle.

The boys raced ahead, thrusting palms at the people closest to the center aisle, trying to see who could get rid of all his palms the fastest.

Petey hung back, too shy to fight his way down the aisle. He looked forlorn as he stood frozen at the rear of the church, clutching his little handful of palms.

Chelsea had an idea. She led Petey out the back of the sanctuary, down the hall, past the nursery, and through the little door to the choir loft, where all the members of the choir were sitting. None of them had palms yet.

"Oh, thank you, Petey!" the ladies cooed as they accepted palms from Petey, his face shining with pride now. He handed out all his palms, then took Chelsea's palms and handed them out, too.

He had one palm left when he and Chelsea joined their parents back in their pew. Danny turned around and gave Petey a friendly, gentle whack with his last palm. Looking thrilled at getting such attention from one of the big boys, Petey happily took his palm and whacked Danny back.

. . .

On Thursday evening that week, Chelsea's family came to church for Communion, to remember Jesus' Last Supper with His disciples. The church was dim, lit only by tall candles on the altar and at the end of each pew. It was like Christmas Eve, but more still and silent and mysterious. Even Danny was sitting quietly with his family.

In their church, anyone could take Communion, including little children. Petey had never taken Communion before, because he was in the nursery during church on Sundays. But Chelsea's parents had brought him with them this evening.

"I don't think he's ready for Communion yet," Chelsea's mother said to Chelsea's father as they sat with Petey, waiting for the service to begin.

"Sure he is," Chelsea's father said. "You're never too young to come to the Lord's table."

The hymns that night were so beautiful that they made Chelsea feel like crying. "Let us break bread together on our knees. Let us break bread together on our knees. When I fall on my knees with my face to the rising sun, O Lord, have mercy on me."

Chelsea was going to see the rising sun in three more days, at the Easter sunrise service, up on the mountain.

The ushers started down the aisle with their little baskets of bread cubes. Mr. Cruz used to be an usher on Communion days. But he wasn't here tonight.

Chelsea's father received the basket of bread cubes from the usher, took his cube, and passed the basket to Chelsea. She took her cube and passed the basket, over Petey's head, to her mother. No one was supposed to eat the bread until everyone in church had been served.

Chelsea's mother took her bread cube, and one for Petey, and tried to pass the basket to the next family.

Petey started to cry. Loudly. "I want bread, too!" he hollered.

"I have one for you," their mother whispered. "See?"

"I want to pick my own!"

"All right." She held the basket where he could reach it. "Just take one."

Petey took a cube. Then he put it back and took another.

"You can't put it back in the basket after you've touched it!" their mother said, forgetting to whisper this time.

Petey grabbed the bread cube he had just put back, plus three others that were near it in the basket. He now had six bread cubes: the one his mother had taken for him, the first one he had taken, the second one he had taken, and the other three. While Chelsea watched in horror, he crammed all six in his mouth at once, without waiting for anybody.

"Oh, well," Chelsea's mother said.

Chelsea held her cube until Reverend Waller said, "Take, eat." As she and her parents swallowed their cubes together with everyone else in the church, Petey began to cry again, "I want bread, too!"

The ushers began to move down the aisles with trays filled with tiny glasses of grape juice. Chelsea's mother whispered to Chelsea's father, "I don't know about this."

After Chelsea's father and Chelsea had served themselves, Chelsea's mother took her own glass of juice and once again tried to take one for Petey. But he reached out and grabbed his own, the fullest one, of course. He spilled it down the front of his little suit jacket before the juice could reach his mouth.

"I take it back," Chelsea's father said ruefully. "You *can* be too young to come to the Lord's table."

But this time Petey was too overwhelmed by what he had done to cry. He just snuggled up against Chelsea.

"Take, drink," Reverend Waller said. Chelsea took one small sip of her juice. Then she shared the rest with Petey. He drank it as carefully as he could, a teensy sip at a time. A few minutes later he was asleep, still clutching the tiny, empty grape-juice glass in his small fist.

Chelsea's parents, on either side of Chelsea and Petey, joined hands behind them. Chelsea felt safe and small, as small as Petey, encircled by their love. She saw Danny's mother with her arm around Danny; he was leaning his head on her shoulder.

"No," Chelsea's mother whispered to Chelsea's father. "*You* were right. Petey was ready. At least, *almost* ready." She dropped a kiss on Petey's sleeping head.

.   .   .

This was the first year Chelsea was going to the Easter sunrise service. Last year, when she had begged to go, her mother had said, "Maybe next year. It's so early, honey. And you know how crabby you are if you don't get enough sleep."

Nothing made Chelsea crabbier than hearing other people talk about how crabby she could be.

But this year her mother had said, "All right. Your father will take you. I'll stay here with Petey."

They were going to have to get up at five and leave the house at five-thirty—a.m.! And the sun would rise while they were on top of the mountain singing "Christ the Lord is risen today!" Nothing could be more Easterish than that.

"Now, don't be disappointed if it rains," Chelsea's mother said the night before. "The Weather Channel is predicting rain."

"It's not going to rain," Chelsea said confidently.

But it did. Chelsea looked out at the droplets running down the dark kitchen windowpane early Easter morning and felt crabby indeed. "How can you have a *sunrise* service if there isn't any *sun*?" she wailed.

"Maybe you should wait till next year," Chelsea's mother suggested.

"No! It will stop raining soon." It *had* to.

Chelsea felt a little bit hopeful as they started driving up the mountain. The rain became a drizzle. Toward the east the sky was gray now instead of pitch black. That was something.

When they got out of the car, they ran through the raindrops to the small cluster of people huddled under the roof of one of the picnic shelters. Reverend Waller was there, in a bright orange rain poncho.

Chelsea felt more hopeful still.

Then someone bumped into her from behind. Chelsea knew who it was before she even whirled around to see. "Danny!" she said crossly. But the ridiculous bunny ears that he was wearing over the hood of his poncho were so funny that she had to grin in spite of herself.

"Happy Easter!" Danny shouted.

"Happy Easter," Chelsea said in return.

With Danny and his brothers there—Jack had driven them with his new driver's license—everything felt more fun and festive. Danny offered Chelsea a handful of jelly beans from his pocket. She took one, to be polite, but she slipped it into the trash when Danny wasn't looking. She hated to think what else had been in Danny's pocket. And she still had her own Easter basket to open with Petey when she got home.

"Hi there, Chelsea," someone else greeted her.

It was Mr. Cruz! Even in the grayness of dawn, Chelsea could see that he had shaved and had combed his thinning hair. He smiled half a smile.

"Connie always loved this sunrise service, rain or

shine. Or snow," Mr. Cruz said. "Many a time I've driven up here Easter morning as the snow was falling."

"It sure is wonderful to see you, Burt," Chelsea's father said, pumping his hand heartily.

The rain had stopped completely now. In the eastern sky the clouds were shifting, breaking, pulling apart like strands of cotton candy.

"Good morning!" Reverend Waller said, officially beginning the service.

"Good morning!" everyone replied.

"Let's start by singing our opening hymn of joy: 'Christ the Lord Is Risen Today.' "

Chelsea didn't need to look at the handout where the words of the hymn were printed. She knew them by heart.

In the east the sky was turning pink. The sun was rising!

Danny's bunny ears quivered in the early morning breeze. Mr. Cruz smiled at Chelsea, a whole smile this time. Chelsea smiled back and kept on singing.

There Is a Season

It was a beautiful Sunday morning in May. The sky was a soft cloudless blue, and the trees were dressed in tender new leaves. Chelsea and Naomi had spent Saturday afternoon picking bouquets of tulips in Naomi's mother's garden. But as she arrived at church clutching her largest bouquet, Chelsea was miserable. The bouquet was for Reverend Waller, because Reverend Waller was going away.

He was going to a different church! A church that didn't have Chelsea in it! He had been Chelsea's minister for her whole life. He had baptized her when she was just a month old. He had given her the special

Bible with her name in it when she was in third grade. He had answered every question she had ever had about God. How could Reverend Waller be going away?

"It can be a good thing to get a new minister," Chelsea's mother had said, after she had broken the news to Chelsea. "A new minister brings new ideas and new ways of doing things."

But Chelsea didn't want new ideas and new ways of doing things. She liked Reverend Waller's ideas and Reverend Waller's way of doing things.

"What's the new minister's name?" Chelsea had asked suspiciously.

"I don't remember her last name. Her first name is Judy."

That was the last straw. Judy! What kind of a minister was named Judy? Ministers didn't even *have* first names. If Reverend Waller had a first name, it was news to Chelsea.

Now it was Reverend Waller's last day. Next Sunday would be the Judy person's first day. No wonder all the blue skies and green trees and bright tulips couldn't make Chelsea's heart sing.

The church was crowded; the pews were full. Everyone had come to say goodbye to Reverend Waller. Chelsea bet the church would be half-empty next week when the Judy person came.

She felt her heart breaking as Reverend Waller greeted the congregation. This was the last time he would ever greet them. She fought back tears as he announced a series of upcoming events. He wasn't going to be there for any of them.

Chelsea was relieved that Amanda was acolyte during the opening hymn. She couldn't have marched down the aisle with tears in her eyes. The thought that Reverend Waller would never again see her be acolyte made a tear wobble past Chelsea's nose.

As their farewell gift to Reverend Waller, the youth bell choir was playing right after the opening hymn. Chelsea didn't feel scared this time as she slipped on her white gloves and picked up her C bell. She was used to performing on the bells by now, and she played each bell perfectly. When they had finished, she could hear Reverend Waller clapping loudest of all. He would never hear Chelsea play the bells again.

"Does anyone have any joys or concerns to share?" Reverend Waller asked at prayer time.

Chelsea's hand went up. She had never raised her hand during prayer time before.

"Yes, Chelsea?"

The familiar gentleness in Reverend Waller's voice was too much. Chelsea couldn't speak over the lump in her throat.

"Our concern," Chelsea's mother said for her, "is that you're going away. We'd like to pray for a safe journey for you and Mrs. Waller, and joy for both of you in your new church."

"Thank you," Reverend Waller said, smiling at Chelsea.

But that wasn't what Chelsea had wanted to pray for. She had wanted to pray that Reverend Waller would change his mind and stay.

The Bible verses Reverend Waller had chosen for the Scripture lesson were from the book of Ecclesiastes in the Old Testament: "For everything there is a season, and a time for every matter under heaven: a time to be born, and a time to die; a time to plant, and a time to pluck up what is planted . . ."

Chelsea knew Reverend Waller meant that there was a time for old ministers to go away and a time for new ministers to come. But why did the time have to be *now?* She hardly listened to the sermon. From the nursery she thought she could hear Petey's wail: good for Petey!

After church, instead of the usual cookies and punch in the fellowship hall, there was a huge all-church potluck dinner. Everyone had brought something to share. Three tables were covered with all kinds of casseroles, gelatin salads, simmering Crock-Pots, and luscious cakes.

Chelsea had considered refusing to eat a single bite. But that would be going too far, even for Chelsea. She got in line, right behind Danny.

Danny was loading his plate as if this were his last meal for a month: three fried chicken drumsticks, a quivering mountain of cherry Jell-O, baked beans sloshing off the edge, a tilting tower of brownies.

When everyone had gone through the line—Danny was already on his second helpings—Reverend Waller stood up to say the blessing. He looked so wise and so kind, so much like God, that Chelsea felt the lump rise in her throat again.

After the blessing, Reverend Waller and Mrs. Waller went from table to table, saying goodbye. "I don't want you to go!" Danny sniffled as Reverend Waller gave him a big hug. That Danny felt the way she did about Reverend Waller's leaving made Chelsea feel a little bit less awful.

Reverend Waller gave Chelsea the same big hug that he had given Danny. He picked up Petey and gave him a tickling squeeze. Then he hugged Chelsea's parents. He had tears in his eyes, too, when Chelsea gave him her bouquet.

And then it was over. Reverend Waller had gone away.

·   ·   ·

When Chelsea came to Sunday school at nine o'clock the next Sunday morning, she didn't see any sign of the new minister anywhere. Maybe she was

planning to make a grand entrance when the service started at ten-fifteen.

In Sunday school they were learning about Noah's ark. Every year they learned about Noah's ark. Teachers probably liked doing Noah's ark because there were so many fun craft projects involving boats and animals. One year they had made animal finger puppets. Another year they had made arks out of shoe boxes.

This year they were making a snack called animals-in-the-rain. First you took animal crackers. Then you covered them with canned vanilla frosting. Then you showered them with sprinkles.

The animals-in-the-rain were delicious. Danny and Angus ate several arkfuls each. But Chelsea couldn't enjoy eating them. In another half hour, the Judy person would be standing in Reverend Waller's pulpit, pretending to be Reverend Waller. Chelsea chomped down angrily on her poor rained-upon animal cracker.

There was still no sign of Reverend Judy as Chelsea joined her parents in their pew.

Mr. Cruz was an usher today. He stopped at their pew and looked down at Chelsea. "The boy who was supposed to be acolyte is sick today. Will you help us out?" he asked.

No, Chelsea was about to say. But her mother said, "Of course."

Sulkily Chelsea went to the back of the church to wait for the opening hymn. The ushers were busy handing out church bulletins. What if Chelsea just slipped away? The opening hymn would begin, and there would be no acolyte. Ha! That would serve Reverend Judy right for not being Reverend Waller.

Maybe they couldn't have church without an acolyte. But Chelsea knew they could. They could have church even without a minister. Chelsea had learned in Sunday school that all you needed for worship was two or three people gathered together in God's name. There sure were more than that here today. The church was as crowded as it had been last Sunday for the farewell to Reverend Waller.

Still, Chelsea didn't have to be acolyte if she didn't want to. She tapped Mr. Cruz on the arm. "I've changed my mind," she said. "I don't want to be acolyte today, after all."

"But, Chelsea," Mr. Cruz began in a pleading voice.

Chelsea knew she was being difficult and unreasonable, but she couldn't stop herself. "I only wanted to be acolyte when we had Reverend Waller."

Danny had come up behind her to get another church bulletin. Chelsea saw that he had already folded his first one into a paper airplane.

"Young man," Mr. Cruz said to Danny, "would *you* help us out this morning and be our acolyte?"

Danny exchanged a look with Chelsea. "If Chelsea doesn't want to do it, I don't want to do it, either."

Mr. Cruz gave a sigh of helpless frustration.

Suddenly Chelsea noticed a small, thin, red-haired woman standing a few feet away. Her hair was wild and curly, sticking out every which way. She looked about the same age as Chelsea's mother. She was wearing slacks and a plain white shirt, carrying a minister-type robe over one arm.

Chelsea was frightened now. This had to be Reverend Judy. And she must have heard everything Chelsea and Danny had said.

But the woman just smiled. "Hi, you two. It's Chelsea and Danny, isn't it? I'm Reverend Judy Jordan."

"How did you know our names?" Danny asked, sounding as scared as Chelsea.

"I have my ways." She lowered her voice and whispered, "I've been studying everybody's pictures in the church directory. Come over here." She led them out of hearing of the ushers.

"Change stinks, doesn't it?" she said in her same friendly voice, as if they were old buddies chatting together. "It's painful, and it's scary, and it stinks."

Well, Reverend Jordan had that much right.

"That's what I think, at least," Reverend Jordan went on. "But then I look around at God's world, the world God made for us, and what do I see? Change everywhere! Changing weather. Changing seasons. Changes in people's lives, from birth, to growing up, to growing old, to death. Everything changes. And do you know what I say to myself?"

"What?" Chelsea said, since Reverend Jordan seemed to expect them to say something.

"I say to myself: Hmmm. God must think change is good for us. God must think change helps us grow into all He wants us to be. Now, maybe I'm right about change and God is wrong. But *probably* I'm wrong about change and God is right."

Reverend Jordan sounded so funny just then that Chelsea felt herself close to a giggle. Danny was grinning, too.

"Give me a chance, you two," Reverend Jordan said. "That seems fair, doesn't it? Just give me a chance. Now, we need an acolyte today. Who's willing to do it?"

"I am," said Chelsea.

"I am," said Danny.

"Okay, you can both do it," Reverend Jordan said. "I'd better go get my robe on. I don't want to be late for church on my very first Sunday."

Reverend Jordan hurried away. Chelsea took one candlelighter, and Danny took another. She wasn't wearing her best dress, and Danny had on his usual jeans with the hole in the knee. But she didn't mind.

Chelsea stood still, thinking. Reverend Jordan said change was good. Chelsea had certainly been through plenty of changes in the last year. She had had her big disaster on the bells; she had had her first fight with Naomi; when Mrs. Cruz died, she had even had her first fight with God. And Chelsea had come to like someone she never dreamed she could: Danny Repetti. Danny wasn't perfect—Chelsea had always known that. But she wasn't perfect either. And that was okay.

The organist started playing the opening hymn: "This Is My Father's World." In the front of the church, Reverend Jordan welcomed the congregation. Chelsea felt her heart ready to burst with happiness.

She turned to Danny to see if he was ready. He gave her a big smile. And Chelsea and Danny carried their candlelighters down the aisle together.